The Blood Red Heiress

The Blood Red Heiress

by

David Keyes

A Cecil Herbert Woolley Mystery

THE HOUSE OF POMEGRANATES PRESS

Published by The House of Pomegranates Press
www.houseofpomegranates.ca

ISBN 978-0-9784543-6-4

Set in Adobe Garamond Pro and
ITC Luna

Garamond is an old style serif typeface originally cut by
Glaude Garamond for the Parisian scholar-printer Robert Estienne in the first part of
the sixteenth century. The Garamond font used in the text of this book was designed by
Robert Slimbach for Adobe Systems in 1989.
ITC Luna is the work of Japanese designer Akira Kobayashi who was inspired by the
designs of the 1930s.

Designed in 2013 by Gillian Holmes of
The House of Pomegranates Press
and typeset in Toronto on an iMac computer.
Copyedited by Jean Nielsen

For Gillian

The
Blood Red
Heiress

Chapter One

CECIL WAS VAMPING on the piano. One could not say he was an accomplished pianist, but he could vamp and at this moment his vamping had no equal. He was in the lobby bar of the Connaught Hotel, a fair-to-high-end sort of place — the kind of place with the kind of bar he liked to frequent and where, coincidentally, most of his clients asked him to meet. He was in fact waiting for one such client, a woman who'd sent her card 'round that morning demanding to meet. She was now 50 minutes and two martinis late. Cecil, trilling down three octaves, gave her ten more minutes by the electric clock above the bar.

Cecil was a consulting detective — wealthy, educated, affected, infuriating, well-spoken, well-dressed, a gentleman, a curious sort, a well-rounded chap, a lover of art, a one-time ladies man, witty and occasionally wise, once attractive and now well worn, functionally alcoholic, kind to animals and a so-so pianist. That gruesome divergence, the Great War, cut short his time at Oxford so he spent his formative years in the air force, demobbing in 1920 with a distrust of power, an absolute loathing of violence and waste, and a passionate, almost obsessive, need for beauty, whimsy and Clemency, the love of his life. He was also recognized around the world for his knowledge of, and some say first-hand experience with, the occult; since starting his consulting practice five years previous many of his top cases involved the dark arts.

She was now 55 minutes late. Continuing to play he signalled the waiter with a nod and with a twitch ordered another drink, his third. Five, he always said, and the evening becomes the drink; four was his gentlemanly limit before nightfall and it was only five minutes to three o'clock.

Just then a very elegant though very flustered woman entered the bar. She wore a celery coloured suit with a tight pencil skirt and a large, black felt hat that did its best to cover a cascade of glorious red hair. Seeing her as the waiter arrived with his martini, Cecil whispered, "That, I believe, is the woman in question. Would you be so kind as to direct her to my booth." He then picked up his drink, drained it and proceeded there himself.

"I am so sorry, I am never late, never. I have never been late. I am so sorry. This has all been too much. I am Anne Carlisle," she said, taking Cecil's hand. She then began to cry. Cecil pulled out a fresh handkerchief and handed it to her. "Thank you," she said and wiped her eyes. She smelled expensive. Gardenias.

"You are here now and that is all that matters. Please do sit down and tell me everything from the beginning."

The bar was starting to get busy. The waiter — a lovely man Cecil always thought — approached. "Another sir? And the lady?"

She looked up, "Hmm, oh, anything, I'm not

particular." (Cecil tried to conceal his disappointment). "Perhaps a dry martini… make sure to chill the glass and wash it with vermouth, none in the shaker, two olives and an pearl onion."

Cecil smiled. "Make that two."

The drinks came and a toast was given, "To absent friends." Cecil began, "So Miss Carlisle, why did you seek me out, me specifically, in a town overrun with consulting detectives?"

"It is rather indelicate and dark," she replied.

"My two favourite words."

"Oh Mr. Woolley," she said and started crying again.

"Please, call me Cecil."

Recovering, she blew her nose and continued, "Mr. Woolley, my fiancé's father is a collector. He has travelled a great deal and obsesses much with the dark arts." She took out a silver case and extracted a thin black cigarette, then turned the case to Cecil. "No, thank you," he said but reached across and lit hers with a lighter that seemed to appear as if by magic.

"Thank you," she said and exhaled a thick blue cloud of clove scented smoke. She rested her cigarette in the ash-tray. Cecil could not help but notice the red lipstick stain from her full lips. She turned her glass absently then continued, "Cyril's father — Cyril is my fiancé — is a lovely man. He is like a character in a children's book, round and short, almost a cliché with his jolly behaviour. He wears a monocle and is forever checking his pocket watch like the rabbit in *Alice in Wonderland*."

"He sounds like quite the character."

"He really is a lovely man. He made his fortune in

steel, specifically for ships."

"I'm thinking he did well for himself in the war."

"Yes, but he hints at a dark guilt because of it. Nightmares. Bouts of drinking alone."

"Ah, yes. It must be a devil's bargain to jus…"

"That's just it, Mr. Woolley! He thinks it was a devil's bargain!"

"Ah."

"I don't know if it's some sort of obsessive self-suggestion as he is surrounded with so much from that world. A majority of his library is devoted to works on demons, the devil and witchcraft. I am beside myself. Lately, when I go into that room there is such a sense of doom. Even with the shutters open there is never enough light and the scent of his incense is always overpowering. It's like a church but a dark church. And lately when I am staying over I hear voices. Cyril shushes me. 'That's just father,' he says but I know there is more to it, I know something is wrong. I am so frightened."

"I am sensing you more than *know* something is wrong."

"That's why I contacted you, Mr. Woolley. Frankly, Cyril's father has become possessed with this idea, this bargain he thinks he made. I had wanted to do something, to try and bring him into the 'light' I guess you could say but I am not religious. I don't believe in the Devil, or God for that matter, so what could I say to him? And Cyril is in such denial he will not let me try anything. My hands are tied." She picked up her drink; it was empty.

"Two more," Cecil said to the waiter and placing his hands on hers said, "Take your time, my dear."

"I was down for the weekend. There was a local fete that both Cyril and I loved to go to. I was convinced we were finally going to set the date for our wedding — we'd been talking about it for ages. It was just the perfect May blossom romantic weekend. When I got to the house that Friday night Cyril opened the door himself. He looked hastily put together, his hair slightly messy, which was unusual as he is always fastidious about his appearance. 'Father is unwell,' he said with a very forced smile and roughly took my bags. 'We'll be alone for dinner, which will be… nice. Cozy. Romantic.' Oh Mr. Woolley, he was not himself. I went to my usual room to unpack, the Red Room, which faces the lawns and down to the sea. I dressed for dinner immediately and went down. Cyril had already started drinking — again so not like him. The house had a terrible edge to it; it was palatable. I have known Cyril and his father since I was a child so I have always been comfortable with both of them and the house. But that night I felt a terrible presence."

"A presence you say?"

"Yes. Evil. Pure evil. There was even a smell. I couldn't quite place it… like burnt meat."

"Grease burning?"

"Yes! That's it. Grease. The house usually smelled, well, of wood or Cyril's lemon cologne or that awful incense of his father's but this was new. It wasn't a cooking smell."

The waiter arrived silently and placed the two drinks on the table, removing the empties. Cecil counted back in his head and said, "Could I get a glass of tepid water?"

"Of course sir."

"And did the father appear that night?"

"No. Cyril tried so hard to act like everything was normal about it. We listened to the Victrola and ate dinner. He kept the conversation light. We talked of the fete and the weekend and a drive we might take but I knew it was forced. He was just keeping me talking, keeping it pleasant and light."

"It could be worse," said Cecil as he sipped. Ah, lovely.

"Yes. But we're not like that. Cyril and I rarely just chat. We've known each other for so long, as I said since childhood, we can and do talk of everything. That night was the first time I got the feeling Cyril was avoiding something. I couldn't stand it. I asked him flat out what was wrong. 'Nothing darling, nothing,' he said. 'Father is… ill. He'll be fine tomorrow. It's been a difficult day.' And then he burst out, 'Can't a man have a bad day? I mean bloody hell Anne, it's not a perfect world, people get sick, things happen, even you must know that!'

It was so terrible. He's never blown up like that. Never. I am usually strong but I was so shocked by his outburst I started to weep. 'Bloody hell!' he shouted and threw down his fork. He took a huge gulp of wine and then dropped his head in his hands and started sobbing. 'Oh Cyril, what is wrong?' I asked. He looked up, his eyes red from the tears, his face drawn and tight. 'It's Father, Anne, he's vanished.'"

Chapter Two

"Good lord," Cecil said. "Vanished?"

"I was so shocked, it was not what I was expecting. 'Cyril,' I said, 'what could you possibly mean?' As far as I knew, his father hadn't left the house or grounds in years, not even to go to the village fete. I asked Cyril to explain. 'I don't know if I can,' he said, disorientated and near to weeping again. 'Father had had a very bad day. A letter came by hand sometime after breakfast that had so distressed him he locked himself in the library and would not come out.'"

She drained her drink and picked a little at the napkin. "Cyril looked at me with a look of desperation and fear. 'Oh Lord, Anne, I think something terrible has happened to him.' Not sure what to do I poured him a stiff drink. Cyril looked up and continued. 'He'd been in the library all day. He does that sometimes, just locks himself in. But today was different. There were noises, hellish otherworldly noises, almost like banshees wailing... no not... oh... I don't know what they were. I also heard voices. Not just his, but men, women... screaming for God's sake!' I'd never seen Cyril so worked up. He continued, 'Finally around six I couldn't take it any longer and just started pounding on the door. Father, I shouted, Let me in! What in the name of God is going on in there? And as soon as I said that the noise stopped. Nothing. Not a sound, just an icy breeze coming from under the door. I took up pounding again, Father, let me in! I ran and got the fire poker and began to smash on the lock. I was frenzied. Oh Anne! I was terrified. Eventually the lock gave way and the door swung open.'"

Here Cyril stopped and seemed to drift into a dream; his eyes became unfocused.

She continued, "I wish you could have seen his face, Mr. Woolley. It was dead white, drained of life, almost inhuman. 'Anne,' he said, 'I have never in my life seen such a sight. Father was gone. There was no one there and all of his books and notes were strewn around the room as if there had been a hurricane. Furniture was knocked over, plants, everything. The stuffing was even torn out from the sofa. His desk was on its side and the carpets were all pulled back and thrown against the wall.' Oh my God, Cyril, what happened I asked him. 'I don't know. I don't know. But that's only half of it. Oh, Anne, it was horrible! On the floor, etched in chalk, was a pentagram and around it two circles with symbols I'd never seen before. There were candles everywhere, black candles that had all guttered out, their wax spilled all over the wood. And the smell! It was so horrible… I can't even describe it.'"

Cecil held up his hand, "A pentagram? Black candles?"

"Yes, Mr. Woolley."

"And he said no one was in the room but he heard voices, many voices?"

"Yes. It was so dreadful but that was not the worst of it; he said that in the middle of the pentagram there was a gold chalice."

"Ah! A chalice… and…?"

"Oh, it is too terrible to relate."

"Please try Miss Carlisle. It could be important"

"Mr. Woolley… it was filled with clotted blood!"

The waiter — such a lovely man — magically appeared. "Another please," said Cecil, "and you, Miss Carlisle? Perhaps to calm the nerves?"

"Thank you Mr. Woolley. Yes, please."

"Did you see the room? When was this?"

"It was two days ago, Saturday. I asked Cyril to show me. He was hesitant at first as it was such a dreadful scene but eventually he gave in and…Oh Mr. Woolley, it was just as he described… horrible! Horrible! All his beautiful books, his furniture, his priceless antiques, all destroyed."

"And there was no sign of the father? Anything? Clothing? A note?"

"Not that I could see."

The drinks arrived. Cecil picked up a martini and handed it to Miss Carlisle. "Here, drink this, it will give your strength. Would you like another cigarette?"

"No, I shouldn't. I am trying to quit, Cyril hates them so. I only smoke when I am nervous."

"I hope I am not making you nervous?"

"Oh no, it's just this horrible event, I feel everything spinning so out of control…"

"Take your time, drink." She sipped her martini. "Were there any other exits to the room that you knew of?"

"I know that house so well and I know, or at least I think I know, all the backstairs and secret passageways. The library had one. It was in the bookshelf but when we opened it, it was so covered in cobwebs and dust there would be no way to pass through without disturbing it. Oh, Mr. Woolley, won't you come down and solve this mystery? It's been two days and Cyril is beside himself. There is still no sign of his father and I fear the house is falling into madness!"

Cecil couldn't help being touched by this poor girl and he certainly was intrigued, more than intrigued actually with the mention of the pentagram and the chalice of blood, but the problem was that at that very instant, in his flat, in his silk smoking jacket (and he imagined not much else), his beloved Clemency was lying on his bed, reading a periodical, probably smoking a cigarette, her pert breasts rubbing against the silk lining of his jacket. He had not seen Clemency in two weeks and... "I'm not sure I have the time, Miss Carlisle. I...."

"Oh, please Mr. Woolley! I have no one else to turn to. Ravensend is not very far and...."

"Ravensend! Wait! Is Cyril's father, Sir Clyde Llewellyn-Jones?"

"Why, yes. Do you know him?"

Cecil checked himself. "Yes, I have heard of him. Hmm, this puts things in a much different light. Yes, I will come to Ravensend." He wrote his address on a cocktail napkin and gave it to her. "I want you to return at once. Do not go back into that room. Tell Cyril that I can come then cable me his answer. If he is agreeable, I will be on the first train down. Do not worry, Miss Carlisle, we will find your fiancé's father and you will have your wedding."

"Oh Mr. Woolley, I cannot thank you enough. I will cable you immediately." She stood up and once again began to cry, "I see nothing but blackness, Mr. Woolley."

Cecil stood up himself and took her into his arms. "There, there. Don't worry, Miss Carlisle. I am on the case and I promise everything will be fine."

"Oh thank you Mr. Woolley, thank you. Expect my cable this evening!" She dabbed her eyes then rushed out of the bar.

The waiter returned. "On your tab sir?"

"Indeed. Tab."

"Are you all right sir? Shall I call you a cab?"

Cecil had never felt better. He had a case to solve and a charming young woman to help and a few days in the country and it was spring. What more could he ask for? Then he frowned; Clemency would understand of course but…. "A cab? Of course not! It's a lovely afternoon, I will walk."

"As you wish sir."

"Thank you, as always, for taking such good care of me."

"A pleasure sir," the waiter said and carefully steered Cecil away from the table he was about to knock over.

Cecil put on his hat, doffed it slightly to the waiter and cautiously made his way to the revolving front door. As he exited he was blinded by the spring sunshine. Like a vampire he stumbled back until his eyes adjusted. Was the sun always that bright? Across the street was a lovely tree-filled parkette where voices seemed to be calling to him. Cecil carefully looked left (forgetting about right) and confidently started to cross, barely dodging the many cars rumbling down the busy street; a dancer could not be as elegant, he thought to himself proudly. When he was across, he lit a cigarette and approached the parkette's ornate fence and gate. He pushed at the gate and it swung open with a squeak. As he entered, the traffic sounds hushed and the temperature dropped slightly. Cecil headed for the bench by the fountain and the bronze stature of a little girl holding a duck. He sat down heavily. "What an extraordinary story," he thought, and then suddenly, quite clearly he saw the cliffs of Dover, gleaming white in the bright sunlight, fall away and the vast, lovely, infinite dark blue of the English channel spread out before him. He ascended high into the sky, then higher still, the rush of the G force in his stomach, the wind blowing hard and cool against him, the clouds high and wispy; the weather fair, so lovely the day. He could see Major Maxwell in the plane next to him. He gave him the thumbs up and set his gauge for France. Suddenly all was dark and he fell into a deep, dark, drunken sleep.

Chapter Three

"'ERE," CAME A voice and with it a hard rapping on his shoe leather. "You can't sleep it off here."

Cecil forced open his eyes; it was dark and it felt as if someone had covered him in sand. "I merely sat down to rest awhile," he said sheepishly to the constable standing above him.

"Mr. Woolley, is it? Now London is a safe city, 'specially in these parts, but who knows what trouble could befall you. I mean sir, what kind of reputation would you, a consulting detective, have if you were sighted by the hoi polloi sleeping off a bender in a public park?"

"Point well taken constable. I am guilty as charged."

"Good, sir. Now let's get you home safely and we'll not talk about this again."

"Thank you constable. You are a gentleman of the best sort."

"Let me…" the officer helped him up, led him out to the sidewalk then blew his whistle, the sound causing Cecil to almost pass out from the shrill expostulation. "Oi, taxi!"

Chapter Four

CLEMENCY DE LA Tour was 34 years old and had black hair that shimmered blue in the right light, and she was the kind of girl who always had the right light. Her skin was the colour of milk, the whitest of pale, as soft as a memory of a summer breeze. In bare feet she stood 5 foot 6 and carried herself with the grace of the dancer she was once was. Her breasts were small and topped by perfect round, pale nipples. Her lips were full, her eyes green, her nose lovely and pointed. When pleased, her lips curled up in a feral manner. She had seven freckles. She wore thick black men's glasses when reading. She preferred not to dress at all but when it was required of her, she always wore black. She smoked cigarettes. She read voraciously. She drank straight gin with ice. She liked to win at Scrabble and usually did. She was impossibly smart. Clemency de la Tour was the daughter of a man high up in the secret service (all very hush, hush) who was somehow related to royalty and very well paid. She never spoke of him though he obviously played an important role in her life, as her mother had died when she was quite young. Although she and Cecil were an item, mentioned often in the social and gossip columns and twice in *Tatler*, Cecil did not know where she lived. They had an agreement; she came and went as she pleased and he never asked. Cecil absolutely adored her, worshipped her actually, so he was fine with this agreement as sometimes he, too, was busy with his work and not available for weeks at a time.

Cecil's flat was once owned by the heir to a food chain who had withered away on opium. Before that it had housed a quite profitable brothel, there was a brass plaque on the door declaring, 'There Are No Prostitutes Here, Please Do Not Knock.' The building sat beside a large park and had been put up late in the last century, giving the flat a certain Victorian comfort. There were servant's quarters and a rabbit's den of rooms that strangely had no right angles. His flat looked out at the oldest part of the park and in the afternoon the sun would stream in through the trees, delicately shaded in the summer or fantastically shadowy in the winter. Cecil filled the place with comfortable furniture, carpets and books (there were stacks everywhere) and art. There were also many instruments of the trade including microscopes, stethoscopes, tarot decks and telescopes — one of which always seemed to be pointed at the apartment across the park — along with two life-sized skeletons, a narwhal tusk and 13 wound and ticking clocks.

"Good God Cecil! You look like something the cat dragged in," said Clemency, curled up in an armchair in Cecil's robe, reading *The Times* as he stumbled through the door.

"I feel more like what the cat threw up, darling. I fell asleep in a park."

"Oh Cecil."

"I know, I know, very unbecoming." He noticed a telegram on the hall table.

"It arrived an hour ago."

Cecil picked it up and ripped it open. 'Matters much worse, come quickly. Anne.'

"I take it our weekend is now scuttled," Clemency said without looking up from the paper.

"I'm afraid so," Cecil replied, loosening his tie. "Do you hate me, darling?"

"Only just slightly. Celia asked me to Billingsgate this weekend for an early match of croquet and since the fates, and that telegram, have conspired to keep us apart, I can now accept. I will not let you off next weekend though; we have tickets to the opera. I know you hate the opera but I do so love you in your tuxedo." Clemency unspooled from the armchair, the robe falling to the floor. "What is in the telegram anyway? A new case?" She walked over and kissed him. "You smell like a dust bin," she said, somewhat lovingly.

"Thank you darling. I have been called worse." He looked longingly at her, sighed then shook his head and crossed the room, removing his clothes piece by piece as he went. "I will have to catch the 8:15 to Bedfordshire; it will be a push but I must bathe and change. Has Benedict arisen yet? I will need help with the packing." Benedict was Cecil's valet. He had peculiar habits, the most remarkable of which was that he only appeared after dusk. "Do see if he is stirring. I feel as if someone has mucked out a barnyard into my head. Could you fix me something, aspirins and a scotch and soda perhaps? Should I eat?"

"Darling, how should I know?" Clemency drawled, picking up the robe. "I've been waiting for Benedict myself. He's the practical one in our relationship."

She put the robe back on and lit a cigarette. She found Benedict in the kitchen, dressed in black, an elegant grey apron wrapped around his waist and oven mitts on his hands. "Ah, Benedict," she said, leaning on the doorframe.

"Madame Clemency, lovely to see you. Will you be staying the weekend?" he asked, walking over to take her cigarette and butt it out in an ashtray.

"I had hoped, Darling, but alas your master has just gotten a case that is taking him off to Bedfordshire, so I am off to Billingsgate."

"Indeed, Madame?"

"He asked me to find you as he's just returned from a date with a park bench and requires…."

"Not again, Madame. Sir is becoming careless. I fear an intervention may be in order."

"Good Lord, Benedict, I can't imagine him sober. Perhaps a fortnight away but not an intervention."

"As you wish, Madame. Did Sir ask for…?"

"Scotch and soda and aspirins and packing. Should we feed him?"

"I have just made scones. Perhaps those and I will fry up some eggs." He poured scotch into a highball glass and siphoned a half of soda, then cracked in an egg and added a few dashes of Tabasco sauce. "Take him this if you will, a bit of the hair of the dog, and I will bring in a supper momentarily."

"You are a saint, Benedict."

"Hardly, Madame."

Chapter Five

As the spires of St Pancreas station receded into the foggy night, Benedict glanced at his watch then snapped it shut contentedly — 8:15 precisely. The train that night was only partially full so they had the cabin to themselves, which pleased them both, as they preferred privacy and abhorred small talk. Cecil liked to talk out the details of whatever case he was working on with Benedict, who he felt had a much cooler head than he. The curtains were pulled back but it was too dark for a view of any sort other than a quickly passed station house or the red of a crossing. The cabin was clean and slightly overheated. Benedict mixed cocktails from their travel case (designed by Georges Vuitton to Benedict's specifications) as Cecil filled him in on the facts of the case.

"Sounds a rum state of affairs," said Benedict after digesting all that was said.

"But what do you make of it?"

"Not really very much, sir. I think we shouldn't come to any conclusions until we see the room, the symbols and, of course, talk to everyone in the house and those nearby."

"Agreed. I just worry when a pentagram figures in it.

It's not something to be meddled with. Pentagrams mean that old horned so-and-so."

"Quite," said Benedict as he expertly poured a drink.

The fog was all enveloping when they arrived. It was a short trip; just under two hours from London through St. Albans, Stevenage, Stafford, Bigglethrope and Audley, but when they reached Beardmore, the last of the Bedfordshire stops, the town was shuttered and asleep. The stationmaster took their tickets and directed them and their luggage to the taxi stand. There was still a early spring chill in the air but it smelled fresh with a scent of new earth and flowering trees. Cecil and Benedict (who was carrying most of the luggage) put up their collars and set forth. Turning the corner of the station they came upon a lone taxicab. Benedict walked forward and approached the cabbie. "Good evening sir, would your taxi be for hire?"

A fetching woman in a chauffeur uniform turned and smiled at Benedict, "It would indeed, sir. Where would you like to go?"

"I beg your pardon madam, I did not.…"

"No offense taken, sir. My name's Emma. I started driving during the War and have come to quite like it. 'Ere, where would you like to go? It's been a slow night I can tell you."

Cecil stepped forward, "Do you know of Ravensend?"

"Know it? I could sell tickets as it's all anyone talks of now."

"Talks of? How so?"

"All the queer goings on, the strange lights. It's been throwing the birds off their flight it has and worse still, we've never had fog like we've had since the Professor went missing."

"You know of that?"

"There are no secrets here, sir."

"Well, can you take us there?"

"Of course, Mr. Woolley," she winked.

"Why, how did you know my name?"

"Like I said, there are no secrets and also my cousin works in the telegraph house." She grabbed the bags and stacked them in the boot. Benedict climbed in the front and Cecil in the back. Emma engaged the car's engine. There was a tremendous sound of grinding gears and screeching and then they were off.

The station was situated in the middle of the town. Beside it, there was an ancient station pub made of fieldstone and a number of very narrow cobblestone streets fanning out in every direction. Emma confidently shot straight down the middle then quite suddenly they were outside the town proper and on a country road. The inky darkness and the dense fog made it quite impossible for either Benedict or Cecil to get a sense of place or where they were — they could have been on the moon. The car roared through the evening silence like some angered beast. Emma seemed to be enjoying herself. "I say," said Cecil from the back, "What else have you heard of Ravensend? Are there any myths or stories told?"

"All I know is what I hear, which comes from my parents talking, or the locals, or what've heard in the taxi. That house has a dark past on it. It's ancient they say. Some say it was built on a druid mound, others say members of the Hellfire Club met there. I've even heard that a witch was burned there. Nothing's happened since I've been alive so I think it's just a lot of superstitious stuff. The Professor and his son Cyril have been as nice and nice can be whenever I've met them. I've run Anne, his fiancée, into town many times and she's a chatty bird. I can't imagine evil in that place. But people speak of it that way and the house has never been able to shake it. And there is that hum...."

Benedict turned, "Hum?"

"Yes, it comes from the forest that surrounds the house. We all hear it. I swear it's true. It started maybe two weeks ago. A low, low, hum. Makes me feel right queer if I get too close to the house."

"And you say," questioned Cecil, "this has been happening for possibly two weeks, no more?"

"Yes, two weeks. We all hear it."

Emma skilfully manoeuvred the taxi through the black of a forest road, the car's headlights barely penetrating the fog. Cecil wished she'd go a bit slower but she seemed confident of the way he said nothing. As the engine was too loud to question her properly he made a mental note to follow up with her in the morning when suddenly the forest gave way and ahead in the distance was Ravensend.

Emma slammed on the brakes and shut off the engine. "Listen," she said and rolled down her window. The cab filled with damp grey air. "Hear it?" Yes, both Benedict and Cecil had to admit there was a very disturbing, very haunting low hum. "Told you," she said then fired up the car again.

Chapter Six

THE FOG WAS so thick that when they pulled up to the front of the house, only the open front door and the windows directly to the left and right were visible. Cyril and Anne were there in the doorway. Emma made a great show of removing the bags from the boot, so Cecil purposely waited before he spoke, paying her more than she asked and giving her his card. "I will be in town tomorrow conducting my investigation. Where will I be able to find you?"

"My parents own the Station Pub. I'll be there if anywhere, or in my taxi, but mostly the pub."

"May I come calling tomorrow then?" Cecil asked, taking her hand.

"Certainly, sir, certainly," Emma blushed then climbed into her taxi and sped off.

"Miss Carlisle," said Cecil walking up to the front door. Extending out his hand to the man beside her, he said, "You must be Cyril. What a terrible time you've been having. Terrible. I am here to help, I promise you."

"Mr. Woolley," said Cyril, taking his hand, the tension in his voice clearly audible, "I am honoured to have you here. Anne has spoken so highly of you. I know we can count on you to solve this bloody business."

"Please, put yourself in my care. This is my man, Benedict," Cecil said as Benedict made his way up the stairs with their luggage. "He is also my assistant in these matters. You must also trust him implicitly. Together, with your help, we will find your father and make everything right again."

"Oh, thank God," sobbed Anne.

"Come in Mr. Woolley, Mr. Benedict, we have rooms prepared for you," said Cyril.

"Before we enter, may I ask a question? The hum…."

"Hum?" they both exclaimed in unison.

"Why, driving up there was a strange hum. Our cabbie said it is all they talk in the village."

"Hum? Preposterous! I've heard nothing, have you Anne?"

Anne shook her head, "No, nothing."

"Are you telling me," Cecil began, "that you cannot…."

Benedict touched his arm, "Sir…."

"Well, we mustn't linger out here in the fog…."

"Yes, of course Mr. Woolley," said Cyril, motioning for them to enter, "Welcome to Ravensend."

Entering, the house seemed calm enough, a fire was roaring in the grate, the lights were all on, but it all rang false and both Cecil and Benedict picked up on this immediately.

Cecil turned to Benedict and whispered, "Are you sensing it?" Benedict nodded.

Cyril took their coats and hats and hung them on the huge hallstand.

"You must be parched, would you like a drink?" asked Cyril.

"Now that is the best idea I've heard all day," answered Cecil.

"I will unpack," said Benedict and took the luggage. "If you would be so kind as to…."

"Oh yes, Mr. Benedict," said Cyril. "I've put Mr. Woolley and you in adjoining rooms; I do hope that is alright. They are the third and fourth doors on your left. The view is of the lawns. Anne will show you the way."

"Thank you, sir," said Benedict.

"Anne, would you mind getting the tray from the kitchen on the way back? Just a few cold cuts I'm afraid, something to stave off starvation."

Anne nodded and led Benedict up the carpeted stairs.

"What a marvellous man," said Cecil. "Now, you mentioned drinks."

"Yes, please come this way." The two men entered a small sitting room. A fire had been lit and its dancing orange light cast eerie and fantastic shadows about the room. Cecil sank into the first comfortable chair he saw. "Here," said Cyril and pressed a button which turned on the table lamps. Instantly the room took on a lovely warm hue. Cyril went to the sideboard and began mixing drinks, "Mr. Woolley?"

"Oh, a gin martini if not too inconvenient. I am quite damp from the fog and need something dry."

Cyril made a double and then poured himself a scotch, adding seltzer from an ornate cut glass dispenser with a lead chain mesh around it. Anne came in with the tray and put it down on one of the low tables.

"I will make a confession to you now," said Cecil after sipping and approving his martini. "I know much more of your father, Cyril, and of Ravensend than I let Miss Carlisle believe."

"But Mr. Woolley, why didn't you tell me when I spoke with you originally?" Anne asked somewhat shocked.

"I wanted to hear everything in your own words."

"But," said Cyril, walking back to the bar to refill his glass, "how have you heard of Father?"

"My good man, in my field you would have to have your head in the sand not to know or have heard of your father and his collection. Ravensend is legendary. I only regret that I am finally coming across your father in such a distressing way."

"Oh, I never thought… of course! Anne told me why she contacted you, how you knew more than most about these matters. It only makes sense that you would know my father and his pursuits. I imagine that world is quite small and close."

"Yes, they do keep to themselves. There is a journal published thrice yearly but because they are dealing in such dangerous fields as the Occult and Demonology, everyone likes to keep it chummy."

"I find that hard to believe," Cyril said placing his glass down. "Wouldn't you want to keep it all very secretive?"

"To outsiders yes, but it's like an old boys club inside. Much bickering and picking over facts. Like any religion or craft guild really, they fight incessantly."

"Fight?!" Anne exclaimed.

"Not in the pistols at dawn sense of the word, more in

an academic too-much-time-spent-indoors kind of way. The old boys would draw blood with their pens but never in a murderous sense." Cecil downed his drink. "I think I'd best do what I came here to do. Or at least begin. May I see your father's study? Am I correct in assuming no one has touched anything since your father's disappearance?"

"Only that first time, when I broke in, and later when I showed it to Anne. I did not want anyone else to see what had happened so I sealed it as best I could."

At this, Anne put her arm protectively around Cyril. "Oh, Mr. Woolley, we cannot thank you enough for coming."

"Yes, Mr. Woolley," Cyril said, exhausted, "thank you."

"I will do my best. Now, can you lead the way?"

Benedict re-joined the party.

"I'm staying here," said Anne, clutching herself, "I can't bear to look at that room again."

"I understand," said Cecil, "You will be safe here and we shan't be long."

With Cyril leading, they walked across the sitting room and into the darkened hall. As they entered the gloom of the passageway, there was an oppressive feel to the air. The temperature began to drop noticeably the closer they got to the library door.

"Sir," said Benedict, "A cold spot. Here."

Cecil stuck out hand, "Yes." He breathed out a cloud of steam. "This is serious."

Cyril stopped and turned, "Here it is. You can see where I smashed the lock." The door was sealed with an x of white sticking plaster; an icy fetid draft came out from the bottom, swirling a low fog into the hall.

Cecil reached into his pocket and pulled out an amber amulet on a silver chain. "And this seal has been here since?"

"Yes. No one has been in or out."

"Okay then," Cecil said and began to remove the plaster. "I cannot tell what is going to happen so let me go first. Wait until I give the all-clear before entering." The men nodded in anticipation of the worst. Cautiously Cecil felt the surface of the door. "Strange, it is warm to the touch." He gave it a slight push but it did not budge. "I'm going to have to give it my all. Gentleman, stand back." With some force he applied his shoulder to the door, which shuddered and terrifyingly seemed to push back.

"Good Lord," Cyril gasped.

"It seems there is some curse or charm at play," Cecil said gravely. "Whatever heinous activities are taking place inside that room, I suspect we are not welcome participants." He reached into his pocket and took out a piece of chalk. "Fire with fire," he whispered and began inscribing a number of curious symbols upon the door. When the last symbol was drawn, what sounded like thousands of skittering feet echoed inside and a wailing, high-pitched moan suddenly took up, nearly deafening the men. A wind began to howl, blowing down the passageway, dangerously knocking objects about. Cecil shouted into the clamour, "*ego praecipio vobis!*" Nothing. "Perhaps it didn't hear me." He shouted again, "*ego praecipio vobis!*" and instantly everything fell silent. Suddenly the door flew off its hinges, splintering against the opposite wall, barely missing Woolley.

Anne came running, terrified, "What's happening? Are you all right?"

"We're fine dear," Cyril responded unconvincingly, "Just stay back."

Cecil turned to her, "Miss Carlisle, this is dangerous as well as…."

"What is happening?!"

Cyril took her into his arms, "Anne, it's going to be okay, we'll find Father, we'll…."

Benedict stepped into the room, "Sir, you'd best come see this."

"What is it, man?" said Cecil, excitedly joining Benedict. "Good Lord!" he gasped. There before him, instead of a library filled with books and furniture, was a room of shifting, blowing sand.

"My God!" said Cyril, "How could this be?"

"Look sir, look!" Benedict pointed to the sand, "Footprints."

"Not footprints, Benedict, hoof prints," Cecil said as he looked down on the marks of two pronounced cloven hooves.

Chapter Seven

CLEMENCY ARRIVED JUST as dinner was being announced — so rude — but as she was expected, the guests used the opportunity for one more cocktail and another cigarette, giving her time to rush to her room to freshen and change. The house's grand dining room was being used; the dinner spread sumptuously over so much silver, gold, fine china and crystal that in the electric light it resembled a jewelled palace. As always, Celia had outdone herself: the wines were vast, varied and heady; the sauces, smooth and exquisite; the courses many and impeccably chosen. Looking at this immense display, deep down, all Clemency really craved was a peach. The guests, of course, were from all the right and/or wrong circles: everyone was charming or decadent or decadently charming; all were fascinating and all were 'in the know.' There were the usual socialites and aristocracy along with bootleggers, gamblers, actors, card sharps, intellectuals, professors, and even composers and writers of the new avant-garde. The conversation bubbled like vintage champagne.

Clemency sat distracted, finding the conversation just so much noise. She was worried. Worried because she was feeling a feeling she had never felt before, a feeling that involved Cecil. Certainly she was fond of him, used to his pattern by now, and such and such, but was she actually becoming attached to him? She shuddered. This was new and she wasn't sure she liked it. Was she growing old, was she mellowing?

"Darling, wasn't it you that was seen naked in the fountain last month at Huntington Glen?" chortled Effie, sitting to Clemency's left, her cigarette burning at the end of a mahogany coloured velvet cigarette holder that must have been a foot long.

"Hmm? Oh… April… no. I was at Capri; it must have been Steffy," Clemency responded distractedly.

Effie blew out a cloud of smoke, "Honestly Clemency, where are you tonight? Steffy, as you very well know, has been in America since last September with that rather well endowed Texan; the one she met at the charity *chemin de fer.*"

"Oh, yes, you're right. I'm sorry, I'm … preoccupied."

"Hmm, is that the word for it? And where is your charming, mysterious Mr. Woolley? I sometimes suspect he is a ghost, a spectre, a pooka. If he were not in *Debretts*, I'd accuse you of making him up entirely."

"Don't be such a stick, Effie. He's busy, he has a job."

"How too dreadful!"

"Yes, well, some must." Clemency looked down Effie's frock at her round, privileged, powdered, buttery Cap d'Antibes tanned boobs and became then and there instantly bored. Thankfully Celia, reaching for her pet rabbit PooPoo (who was leaping about the table as part of the centerpiece), leaned in too close to the candelabras and set her feathered tiara aflame, which cut short the dinner, sending everyone to the games room for coffee, conversation and, more importantly, more booze.

When no one was looking Clemency, who had been to Billingsgate more times than she could remember, took her rather strong martini and made her escape. She slipped off her shoes and padded across the marble, polished hardwood and plush carpets of the house's many darkened rooms, all filled with priceless furniture, antiques and paintings, all reeking of money, damp rot and dog. She felt lonely, very much the only girl in the world. Unseen clocks ticked on mantles while somewhere in the distance, a grandfather clock struck eleven. She loved this huge haunted house, so vast and so quiet and so easy to be alone in.

She finished her drink as she approached the library door. She carefully turned the huge brass handle and went in. Moonlight was flooding the room. This was a more recent addition to the ancient part of the house, having been designed and built in 1793 by John Nash who, on a break from designing the prisons at Cardigan, found himself transfixed by the house's strong lines and the pleasant sight of a field of meandering sheep before it. He stayed six months, *pro bono*, impregnated the then lady of the house and designed the lovely room the moonlight was now flooding and Clemency was now standing in. The virile round structure soared five stories, topped by a glass dome. Bookshelves circled up into its heavens, each level ringed by a balcony that could only be reached by an ornate winding stairway. The ground floor contained an odd assortment of dangerously comfortable sofas, all placed under the dome to favour the sun by day and the starlight by night. A fire in the lavish fireplace could warm the room quite nicely, and hidden by a sliding false front disguised as a collection of bound-in-calf liturgical books (Clemency being one of the few to know this) was a very well stocked bar.

Clemency walked over and slid back the front to refill her drink. There was no ice so it was warm, but it was potent and that was all that mattered. Feeling quite tipsy, she placed her glass on a side table and fell into one of the chairs. Above her, *Draco*, *Ursa Minor* and *Camelopardalis* looked down approvingly. She was grateful for the silence, as she needed to collect her thoughts, fuzzy though they were. Damn it, she mused, she was going to have to admit it, she was in love.

Silently from the shadows a dark shape slid into the moonlight. Clemency screamed. It was only Asquith, the butler, with a telephone on a silver tray.

"Oh good lord, Asquith, you scared the wits out of me."

"Terrible sorry ma'am. Telephone. For you." He placed the phone on the table by her drink, then ran the long cord over to the wall and plugged it in. "Will you be needing anything else, ma'am?"

"No, Asquith, no … Thank you."

She picked up the cold black Bakelite receiver.

"Hello?"

"Darling." It was Cecil. "I needed to hear your voice."

"Woolley, darling, where are you? I thought you were in Bedfordshire?"

"I am awash in Bedfordshire. I am also in a room decorated like a French cat house and, it appears, quite,

quite drunk."

"Oh, Woolley, I do worry about you."

"Do you darling? Do you worry? Do you miss me also?"

She paused. "Yes, I am afraid to admit it, but I do."

"Darling. I think I need you. Loath to admit it, I think I am quite terrified."

"What?!"

"I don't want to discuss it this way, over the telephone, but I truly think I need you here. Can you come?"

"Woolley, is it that bad?"

"Worse than bad. I think I have, after all these years, finally come up against the true evil one — the Dark Prince himself!"

Chapter Eight

"Sir." It was Benedict.

"Wha..time is it?" winced Cecil.

"5:30 sir, dawn will be soon."

"Oh."

"I've laid out your clothes for the day...."

"Yes, Benedict, you are a prince, a prince...."

"Sir, I thought you should know that Miss de la Tour is..." he cleared his throat, "asleep at the end of your bed."

Cecil shot up and looked down. "Good Lord!"

"She came in around 3 a.m. saying you telephoned her, begging her to come. She was exhausted and distraught about something you had told her; she was also covered in leaves. She demanded I take her to your room and then upon arrival instantly fell asleep, as you see her now. I thought I'd best warn you before the breakfast gong is struck."

"Quite right Benedict, quite right. Decency and...."

The room began to blush with dawn colour. "I will leave you then sir."

"Thank you," said Cecil and Benedict hushed out of the room. He lay back down and thought, "This is a pickle," then, "she came when I asked." His heart swelled and in complete happiness he fell back asleep, dreaming his long dead cat Cristobel was pressed up beside him, taking up all the bedclothes. When he awoke, he found Clemency wrapped around him, fully dressed and drooling slightly. Looking at her he realized he had never seen a more beautiful creature in his life, he feared his heart might explode with love.

Clemency stirred then opened her eyes, "Darling."

"Darling."

"I came when you asked."

"Oh Clemency, so you did. What did Celia say?"

Clemency wriggled closer, "I was so rude, I left a note with the butler and just left. I am glad really. I had no idea who was going to be there and honestly Cecil, I didn't want to play croquet."

"Of course not, darling. Of course not."

"Darling, what you said over the telephone, what did you mean?"

"You know why I am here? Well, I think," Cecil reached over and lit two cigarettes, handing one to Clemency, "I think Cyril's father actually struck a bargain with the... Devil. I think old Mr. Unlucky has been here; may still be here, somewhere, in the house. I think, and please don't mention this to the household, I think the Prince of Darkness has collected our Lord Llewellyn-Jones and taken him off across that old river Styx."

Clemency delicately plucked a flake of tobacco off the tip of her tongue, "Good Lord, Cecil, you can't be serious."

"I'm afraid I am." Cecil exhaled a cloud of smoke.

"But how can I help? What can I do?"

Cecil smiled, "Love me."

"I can't see how that can help you win over the Horned One."

"I need you to help me act like everything is as if it isn't. If I am going to find Cyril's father, I am going to need an atmosphere where no one suspects what I suspect. I need you to be your charming distracting self while I, and I never thought I'd ever get to say this, while I call forth the Prince of Darkness and demand a meeting."

"But how will you do it?"

"Haven't the faintest."

From far away there was the sound of a gong.

"Breakfast," said Cecil. Looking at Clemency, he pondered, "Darling, how am I going to explain you?"

"I would hope you wouldn't have to. Can I not remain a mystery?"

"You will always be a mystery, my darling, the most magical of mysteries, the mystery that all mysteries are made upon. However, it is your presence here that I need to explain. I mean you are in my bedroom."

"Oh darling, you are so bourgeois. No one cares about those Victorian mores anymore. Honestly Cecil, what century do you come from?"

"I would hope whichever still has gentlemen concerned of a lady's honour!"

"You are my muffin," Clemency sighed, and kissed him passionately.

"Well then, freshen up and prepare yourself for a country breakfast."

"Good Lord! Not more organ meats."

Chapter Nine

CECIL AND CLEMENCY descended the stairwell and joined their hosts in the aptly named Breakfast Room. It was certainly a delicious day. The windows were open and a breeze so delicately scented of spring flowers and newly turned earth streamed in. The sun was warm and the heat optimistic. It was hard to believe there was such evil in the house. The room's walls were fussily papered with heavy Victorian patterns, yet that did not take away from the loveliness of the space and its view of the lawns and forest. Cecil noticed right away that Anne and Cyril took no comfort from the cheery spring weather; they looked drawn and yellow as they sat at the table. Although their plates were full, they just picked at the food. Cyril had noticeable dark rings around his eyes and Anne's face was stretched tight.

After a brief, awkward silence Cecil cleared his throat, "Good morning, you'll notice there is another joining us. I do so hope you don't mind. Cyril, Anne, this is Clemency de la Tour. She arrived late last night. Benedict let her in. I hope you don't mind."

"Why, is this the Clemency you talked in length about last night?" said Cyril straining to be cheery.

"The same," responded Cecil, somewhat chastened.

"Then welcome. Please, we're not formal in the morning, everything is on the sideboard, just tie on a nose bag and join in."

"Yes, please join us," said Anne gesturing to the table.

"Thank you," said Clemency. Cecil quietly sighed, relieved that no one really took notice, then handed Clemency a warm plate, "Darling… plate."

Cecil and Clemency went to the sideboard and sampled, then joined Cyril and Anne at the table. There was a fresh copy of *The Times* on the table but as no one had touched it, Cecil felt rude in wanting to. They ate in relative silence.

"Didn't see Benedict this morning," Cyril said, trying to make conversation.

"No, he keeps nocturnal hours."

"Odd."

"A dragonfly draws water out of its own rectum for sustenance. Now that is odd."

Clemency pushed Cecil, "Cecil!"

"Sorry darling, product of too much reading."

Silence.

Then Anne cried, "What are we going to do? I can't stand this waiting!" She dropped her cutlery and began to weep.

Cyril, trying to comfort her, reached over and placed a hand upon her arm. "Oh darling, we must have hope. Mr. Woolley, do you have any ideas? How shall we proceed?"

Cecil wiped a bit of egg off his lip with a crisp white napkin. "I want to spend the day in the study. I'm going to have to move that sand, or at least enough that I can get a glimpse of the writings you saw on the floor. I'll need a shovel or some such thing."

"Of course, whatever we have here is at your disposal."

"Excellent. And I'd like your help, Cyril. Clemency…."

"You're not expecting me to shovel, are you?"

"Darling, no. Could you run the car into town with Anne? This will be quite boring and it might be nice for the two of you to get away for a bit."

Anne looked up, "Oh, I would be terrible company."

"Nonsense," said Clemency. "It seems a glorious day, let's see what mischief we can get into."

Anne smiled a faint smile, "I will try my best."

Cecil caught Clemency's eye and smiled, then mouthed, "Thank you darling."

Chapter Ten

AN HOUR LATER Cecil stood on the third floor terrace, watching the girls drive off in Cyril's red, low-slung 6C 1750. He lit a cigarette. "There is honestly no one who can compare," he mused, watching Clemency at the wheel. He looked down and noticed Cyril at the foot of the steps, lingering long after the car had moved out of sight. Cecil dragged on his cigarette and watched fixedly until Cyril turned and walked slowly back into the house.

Descending the stairway he found Cyril in the landing alcove staring into space. "I say, old chap, buck up now! We'll get to the bottom of this. I honestly feel your father is still alive."

"I know, Mr. Woolley. I can feel it too. It's just so damned difficult keeping positive. It's been such a strain since Father turned in on himself and now this disappearance. Honestly, I don't know how much more I can take! I mean what in blazes is going on?"

"That's what I'm here to find out, and find out I will. Now, you mentioned a place where we can find shovels and that sort of thing?"

"Yes, the shed. It's attached to the mudroom by the scullery; come, I'll take you through one of the passages.

You might find it interesting."

Cyril walked over to a small oak cupboard mounted on the wall by the grandfather clock. He reached into his pocket and took out his fob. Attached to it was a key and with that he opened the cupboard door. Inside were a series of hooks with ornate paper labels pasted above them, some quite old and yellowed; on each hook hung an ancient-looking key. Cyril selected one and then shut and relocked the door. He pointed by using his chin, "This way," and headed to a low door in the wall at the base of the stairwell.

"I used to use it all the time when I was younger, quicker than the stairs," said Cyril as he put his hand on the handle. He opened the door and a damp, cool breeze came billowing out. "Mind your head, the door is low. Not sure whom this was designed for, certainly not for servants as you would think. It was fine when we were kids but now it's a bit cramped." Cyril bent down and entered the passage, Cecil followed. The walkway was just raw lath and plaster. There was, however, a runner carpet and now and then a wall sconce with a dim electric light. There was also an overwhelming smell of rot.

Cyril turned to Cecil, "There has always been that smell. It's not in the house just here in these passages. They are supposed to lead out to the grounds but I only used them when I wanted to get to other parts of the house. It gives me the willies on bad days."

"This is absolutely fascinating, though common in houses such as these. Where are we going exactly?"

"Here, on the left, these stairs will take us down to the...."

"Damn!" Cecil hit his head on an arch in the tunnel.

"Like I said, not made for a grown man. Here...." Cyril gestured to stairs, which circled down into darkness.

Suddenly a low hum seemed to come from all around them. "Good heavens!" exclaimed Cyril.

"What in the...." Cecil hissed as the lights went out plunging them into darkness. Cecil lit a match, illuminating a tiny patch around them. "Cyril, old chap."

"Yes."

"I don't think that's the plumbing. We need to get out of this space."

"Agreed."

The match went out. Cecil lit another. "As quick as...." Suddenly a ghastly moan erupted, shaking the walls and causing the ancient plaster to rain down upon them. A voice angrily shouted, "Leave now! Leave this house!" Cecil dropped the match and covered his ears. "Leave now or his father is doomed. Doooommmmed! Hear what I say, no good will come from your meddling in what you don't understand. Go now .... GOOOOOOOOOOO!" A powerful wind then came up causing dust and debris to whip at them painfully.

"Cover your eyes!" Cecil yelled. They were both blown back. The wind howled like a tempest, crashing through the space for what seemed an eternity and then it stopped.

"What in hell was that?" Cyril said dusting himself off.

"Who in hell might be the better question; I don't suppose anything like that has happened before?"

"Absolutely not."

"Are you okay? One piece, no bones broken or misaligned?"

"I'm fine, as fine as I can be, considering. Look here, it knew you were here."

"Yes… well…."

The electricity came back on.

"Ah. The light. Let us move out of here with great haste."

"Watch me fly!" Cyril leapt down the stairs two at a time with Cecil following close behind. At the bottom they came to another small door, similar to the one they entered. Cyril gave it a push and suddenly they were in a sunny, large and very quiet Victorian kitchen.

Cyril went over to the icebox and opened it. He took out a carafe of water and placed it on the kitchen's large wooden table. He then took down two tumblers from the glass-fronted cabinet and poured water for each of them, saying quietly to himself, "Could use something stronger." He drained the glass and put it down.

"Have you heard that hum or anything like that voice before?" Cecil asked.

"No. I'd have told you about it. I mean honestly, that was bloody terrifying."

"Yes, well, that's the hum that the villagers have been hearing. Whoever it is or whatever it is they want us out, me in particular."

"I suppose this has to do with Father and his damned meddling in the occult. Guess he was better at it than I gave him credit for."

"Cyril, you do realize that your father was actually… sorry… is actually quite well known? Have you not read any of his articles?"

"What? Articles? Well, he did ask me to read some but I thought them just so much mumbo jumbo. Bosh really. You can't tell me that in the year 1928 such things exist?"

"Oh my dear Cyril, the things your father meddled with are older than time and will be here long after the human race blows itself to kingdom come." Cecil paused, "The 'great' war I thought would put an end to it all but it just stirred the flame. Now we have greater and more efficient killing machines. The dark satanic mills Blake talked of, they're still here, belching fire, lighting the countryside sky. We did not build Jerusalem we blew it to bits. Here in England, most of what you call the occult is ancient and majestically earthy, like giants... mostly benign giants like the seasons, nature. However, there is also an evil side, the world Prospero locked inside the petrified tree. Unfortunately, I think your father found that world with its easy power and unchecked greed. But like everything in nature, deeds echo back and in the world of the occult, it comes back three times stronger. Your father, I suspect, has made some sort of bargain and I have the feeling he is now being asked to pay."

"Good Lord, you can't be serious!"

"I wish I weren't." Cecil filled his glass and drank. "Come... shovels... we've got a desert to clear out before the day is done."

Chapter Eleven

THEY FOUND THE shovels where Cyril said they'd be and grabbing two, along with a broom for good measure, they headed back into the house. Despite Cecil's dislike of naked sunshine, he regretted having to go back inside; it was too glorious a day to be wasted on evil. The gilly-flowers were in bloom. But he was here to clear the place of evil so the flowers would have to wait.

The house was deathly quiet with the girls gone, and icy cold. They found the wreckage as they left it from last night; the hallway still covered in bits of wood and pieces of unidentifiable bric-a-brac. A strange eerie calm had settled over the space. Then they noticed the library door, back on its hinges and showing no signs of the previous night's maelstrom.

Cecil gestured Cyril out of the way. "Best stay back, old man, while I try the door." Prepared for the worst, Cecil made his way towards the door when suddenly it swung open on its own.

"Be careful," whispered Cyril, "who knows what…."

"No need for the worry," Cecil said. "Have a look."

"Good lord…" gasped Cyril for the room was completely back to normal. There was no sand, no overturned furniture. The books were on their shelves, the plants back in their pots, the sofa in perfect shape. The windows were shut and the room once again smelled of incense and tobacco. In fact, it was as if time had moved back by months, even years. But it was only an illusion for there on the floor was the pentagram with its circles of symbols, the dark piles of candle wax and the gold chalice, though now overturned and empty.

"Well I didn't expect this," said Cecil. "This is certainly turning out to be one of the most unusual cases I've been on."

"Have you seen the symbols before?"

"Oh yes. That's Enochian."

"Enochian? Is that a language like Greek or...."

"No, this is no common language. It is the language of the angels; a language dictated to and written down by John Dee, Queen Elizabeth's astrologer. It has never been deciphered but occultists believe these symbols carry important mystical powers, summoning powers."

"Good God!"

"And it seems your father was using them for that very purpose."

"To summon?"

"Yes, look around. The pentagram, the safe circle, brick dust across the entrance of the room, the candles; these are all tools." He picked up the chalice and looked at the residue. "Blood," turning to Cyril, "Lost a cat lately?"

"Cat, no, why?"

"Hmm. Damn, I didn't bring the journal." Cecil walked over to the bookshelf, carefully avoiding stepping in the circle. "If his taxonomy matches...hmmm...

spells… hermeticism… tarot… Mrs. Beeton… neo-platonism… kabbalah… gnosticism… alchemy… astrology… numerology… themema… theosophy… divination… aha! Angel languages. Now, does he have… no… no… no… I can't believe he wasted his time with… no… no… Ah! Here it is. The 1582 version!" Cecil paused. "I fear I may weep. He has an original copy." He opened the book and inhaled. "Just think of it, what a stupendous thing."

"Steady on," exclaimed Cyril.

"Yes, sorry, hmm, let me see…," Cecil began to flip through the pages. "My edition is different. Now… ah… here it is." Cecil began looking at the symbols inscribed on the floor, comparing them with the symbols in the book. After fifteen or so minutes of this he slammed the book shut and placed it on a desk.

"Well?" said Cyril. "Well?"

"I'm afraid it's not good. I'm not saying I'm an expert on Enochian but I fear — and brace yourself — I fear your father really did make a Devil's bargain."

"What are you saying, man? That my father actually sold his soul to the Devil? I can't believe that!"

"Whatever you do or don't believe, all this indicates that your father struck a supernatural deal and it looks like he is making every effort to get out of paying it, or … asking for an extension."

From behind them a voice said, "An extension for what?"

"Clemency," Cecil shouted, turning, "you mustn't come in here, it is too dangerous!"

"Oh darling, it doesn't look dangerous at all."

Cyril looked up, "Where's Anne?"

"Here I am," Anne said, walking into the room. "Poor Clemency tried to amuse me but I fear I was no joy. I became so anxious I just had to come home. We were in the teashop when something came over me; I had to come back. I almost wrenched poor Clemency's arm out of her socket and made her drive us here."

Suddenly there was a creak. Anne let out a gasp as a section of the bookshelf slid back and out of the darkness stepped Sir Clyde Llewellyn-Jones!

"Father!" cried Cyril.

"Stay back, Cyril," Sir Clyde shouted, then threw some powder on the floor that exploded in green smoke. "All of you. Stay back. This is not a child's game!" Another explosion. "I know what I am doing, I am an expert!" He waved his arms and a great burst of thunder rocked the room. "I have dealings with the Lord God Lucifer himself. I don't have time to shilly-shally with the likes of meddling amateurs!" he pointing to Woolley. "Get out of my house. Get out at once!" Another explosion of thunder, the room was now practically lost in a green haze.

Cecil thought Sir Clyde overly theatrical, then realized the man had been using the oldest trick in the magicians handbook. "God lord, Anne!" Cecil shouted, "Get out of the...." But it was too late, Sir Clyde had grabbed Anne by the arm. "My dividend! You," he bawled, "shall be the Blood Red Heiress of my Infernal Bargain!" Anne let out a blood-curdling scream as suddenly the room fell black.

When the light came back and the green smoke had cleared, there were two less people in the room.

"He's got Anne! Oh my God! Anne! He's taken my Anne!" screamed Cyril helplessly.

Chapter Twelve

THEY WERE ASSEMBLED in the Evening Room. A fire had been lit to lessen the evening's chill and in a fruitless attempt to banish the shadows all the electrical lights were ablaze. It was cocktail hour and exhausted by the day the remaining members of the party, still somewhat in shock, tried their best to settled in. It was a lovely and comfortable room, the biggest in the house, with wood paneling and wall tapestries advantageously placed to stop the drafts so characteristic of great English homes. The stone fireplace was large, with carved heads that held up the mantle, their eyes cleverly glowing with the flickering of the fire. The room smelled of warmed dust and smoke, mixed with the scent of tobacco and Clemency's perfume, a musky patchouli she mixed herself.

Benedict, in a crisp white jacket and black trousers, was frowning; after checking the stocks, he was disappointed to find there was only Brokers gin; he would have to make do. First, he swirled dry white vermouth around the already chilled shaker and dumped it. Then he measured six ounces of gin, three dashes of absinthe and a dash of bitters. Reaching for the ice, he frowned again. The ice was of the modern variety, made from the new ice cube trays that were now so fashionable, trays that made the ice all hard surfaces and uniform. Oh, how he hated the uniformity of modernity. Ice should be odd-shaped with soft rounded corners. He sighed quietly. He took his bar towel and wrapped it around the silver shaker (the shape of which was not to his liking), and gripping it firmly with one hand on the stopper and one under-neath, began shaking vigorously. The trick was to shake three times forward (which wakes up the gin) and then two side-to-side (which slivers the ice and infuses it into the alcohol) – three and then two, three and then two; the art was not to look foolish while doing this. Once the shaker was crusted with frost, Benedict poured three perfect martinis into three chilled glasses and put them on a silver serving-tray. He walked the ten paces to the sofa where Woolley was stretched with his stocking feet under Miss de la Tour's bottom and served the drinks.

"Ah Benedict," said Cecil and, holding up one hand for silence, he sipped. "Perfection."

"For goodness sake," yelled Cyril, "must we just sit here acting like nothing has happened while Anne is somewhere, God knows where, being sold off as a devil's concubine?! This waiting cannot be helping her. There must be something we can do!"

"Waiting, my dear Cyril, is an activity. To wait: I wait, you wait, we wait — we are in fact doing something, how-ever passively."

Clemency pulled at Cecil's foot. He frowned, "For-give me. There are things I need to tell you… Please, I am unsettled until you drink." Cecil raised his glass, "Ab-sent friends," and the three drained their glasses. Instantly

Benedict began shaking another.

"Tell us what?" demanded Cyril impatiently.

Cecil stood up. Benedict brought him another drink on the silver platter then continued on to Clemency and Cyril. Cecil raised his hand again and sipped. "Aaah." Turning to Cyril, he began. "Now, the facts are these. Your father made an awful lot of money during the war, an inestimable amount according to my sources. There was much talk in the city of dirty dealings and contracts falling into his lap far too easily; the procurement process of three bids, some said, was not done. Now this could all be bitter apples on the part of the business community but there was too much talk coming from too many quarters. The strange thing was that nothing was done and by the time the war ended, your father was very rich indeed and everything had been forgotten. However, after the war your father began publishing some very detailed and very dangerous articles about the occult with a knowledge no amateur ought to know. I suspect he, as an enthusiast, could not hold back sharing what he had learned, even boasting a little. One article I remember from '23, if I am correct, talked of actual contact with demons. Not just the theory but genuine contact. Very dangerous and ancient incantations that used the principle of...."

Clemency downed her drink. "For goodness sake, Cecil, stop acting like a bloody professor and get to the point."

Cecil raised an eyebrow. "Cyril, a mysterious letter is delivered to your father and he falls into a funk, locking himself in his study. Voices are heard. Incantations. Violence. And then he disappears. Then he reappears and takes your fiancée as part of a bargain he..."

"Bargain?!" cried Cyril. "You keep talking of this bargain..."

"My dear boy! Once again... your father has struck a bargain with the Devil and the Devil has come to collect. I am of the belief that he is offering your lovely Anne as collateral so he can extend the contract."

"Oh my lord, Cecil, like white slavery!" gasped Clemency.

"Something of the sort."

"That's daft! How do you expect me to believe that?" Cyril shouted, gulping down the rest of his drink.

(Benedict began shaking a third)

"Believe what you will," continued Cecil, "but your father believes it; believes it enough to take Anne a prisoner; believes it enough to hide within the walls of this house from some foe we cannot see. As crazy as it sounds... oh, thank you, Benedict." As he picked up the icy martini from the silver tray he again held up his hand for silence.

Clemency punched his arm. "Cecil, if you are going to do that each and every time you sip a cocktail, I will not live with you ..."

"Ah. Perfection. Darling, I am trying to focus... collect the facts... the old dangling threads."

"Harrumph," Clemency grunted.

"Now, where was I? Ah, yes... as crazy as it sounds, since the bargain was struck here, the window, door, portal was opened here and so the Devil, the Prince or whatever you'd like to call him, must return through that fenêtre and either collect his dark prize or renegotiate the terms. Sadly, I cannot imagine someone coming away from the table a winner when trying to negotiate with the Devil — do you know one of his names is The Adversary? Like most 'banks,' he does not like to lose and because I suspect he was not happy with your father's original terms, he gave him new ones."

"Good Lord… Anne."

"Yes, I'm afraid Anne."

"Oh my God!" Cyril sobbed. Clemency went over and put her arm around him. "My God!"

"Don't give up just yet. I went into the study after Anne's disappearance and did some light reading. I found some very interesting things indeed. Knowing your father will have to return to the study to complete the *négociation*, I also took the liberty of removing two items I know he will need — his summoning bell and his Grimoire, which he is powerless without. I also erased three symbols from the circle on the floor and by doing so broke the spell so it is no longer sound. No demon will enter that circle now, especially if there is no bell to summon and no words to speak."

"If he can't summon the Devil, what will become of Anne?!"

"Cyril, don't worry. She is alive and at the moment she is the only thing keeping your father from eternal damnation."

"So what do we do?"

"Yes, Cecil," Clemency said, slightly exasperated. "Could you get to the part where we actually do something to save Anne?!"

"We wait."

"What?! Wait!" cried Cyril. "Haven't we waited

enough?"

"We wait." Cecil replied calmly. "At midnight your father will appear in his study with Anne. The deal will fall through and we will take her and your father and... well...." Suddenly a gong sounded. "Ah, that must be dinner, I could eat a metaphorical elephant!"

Chapter Thirteen

THE SHIP'S CLOCK mounted on the dining room wall struck the quarter, 11:15. They were long at dinner, Cecil having picked every fact he could from Cyril about his father. To keep their minds fresh, Cecil insisted they drink clear liquids so no red wine, only straight gin was called for. Clemency yawned loudly. Cecil looked at her, his heart swelling with adoration. "Sleepy, Darling?"

"I'm afraid so, it must be the country air mixed with all this intrigue."

"Well, it won't be long now. I think actually we should quickly change into more practical clothing and meet back down stairs as soon as possible. Cyril?"

"I'll be but a moment," he said, and rushed from the room.

"Enthusiastic," Cecil said, then leaned over to Clemency and kissed her.

"Are you always this pompous on a case?" She asked.

"Oh no, I'm usually much worse."

"If I am to spend any time with you, promise me you will not take me on any more of your cases."

"I promise Darling, I promise."

The three of them assembled at 11:35 in the drawing room. There were paintings on the wall dating back to the beginnings of the Llewellyn-Jones family; in fact there was a Llewellyn and a Jones. The far wall faced west and was comprised of an enormous picture window broken into squares. There was a bench in front of it festooned with pillows. Through the window one could see the west lawns and past that the ornate pond and oriental bridge, all glowing a ghostly silver white in the moonlight. Benedict joined them.

Cecil began, "Now, I need you all…."

"I say!" Cyril cried out pointing, "Isn't that Father crossing the lawn?"

"Good Lord, it is!"

Clemency ran to the window, "What's he carrying?"

"Rope, it looks like," Cyril responded.

"Oh God," Cecil cried. "Rope! Quick, everyone after him!"

"What is it, what is it?" panicked Clemency.

"The blighter! I underestimated him, quick!" Sir Clyde was moving quickly; he was across the lawn and onto the bridge before they got out the door. They got as close as they dared.

"Quick, here behind this topiary," whispered Woolley, "we can watch your father. Keep as quiet as you can."

"What is going on?" Cyril asked. "I'm so confused. Why don't we just grab father and make him take us to Anne?"

"It's not that simple. We have to let this play out. We have to let him lead us to the bait — forgive me — lead us to Anne. We can't just take her; it could do her harm.

She could be under a spell."

"Darling," Clemency tugged on Cecil's jacket. "What is happening, what is he doing?"

"I've only read about this but I believe he is trying to summon without the bell. It's very dangerous doing it this way but I think Sir Clyde is desperate. He must have seen what I did to his circle, noticed his missing Grimoire."

There was a horrible stillness to the clear night. The chilly air was scented with a mix of early night-blooming stock, new grass and the brackish smell of the ornamental pond; it was also damp and they were slick with moisture and perspiration, an uncomfortable combination. An eerie mist rose off the water. Sir Clyde stood alone on the bridge. He had lit candles at each end and had drawn a white line with chalk connecting them. He reached into his shirt and pulled out a medallion and held it to the moon. They could hear his voice chanting but could not make out what he was saying. It was rhythmic and low, very guttural. Above, clouds appeared where there were none before and the moon came in and out of view. The shadows on the lawn elongated and shortened rhythmically, it was terrifying to behold. Clemency latched onto Cecil for safety.

"Look," said Cyril. "Father's finished chanting; what's he doing now?"

Sir Clyde bent over and picked up the coiled rope. One end he put under his foot and the other he very slowly lowered into the water. The rope dangled loosely and when it hit the water began to move with the slow motion of the current under the bridge. Sir Clyde let more rope into the water then stopped. He looked down and began to intone, "Lord Satan, hear me. I summon thee. I summon thee."

"Satan is in the lake?" asked Clemency.

"Wait," Cecil said. And they continued to wait.

"Lord Satan, hear me. I summon thee. I summon thee." Sir Clyde's voice was beginning to crack from exhaustion. "Hear me! Hear me!"

Suddenly the rope became taught; it went from lazily drifting under the bridge to stiff and straight down into the water.

Sir Clyde continued his evocation, "Satan! I summon thee! I summon thee!"

Suddenly Clemency put her hand on her mouth for out of the black water, like an ancient primordial insect, what looked like a man began climbing slowly up the rope and onto the bridge.

Cecil was beside himself. He took out a silver flask and took a long swig. "It worked. I've only read about it but it worked, fascinating," he whispered.

Clemency was paralyzed with fear. Cyril just stood, staring in disbelief. The figure was too far away to make out clearly but he was tall and wore what looked like a dark suit. He seemed very angry and began yelling and gesturing to Sir Clyde. Sir Clyde fell to his knees and began kissing the thing's feet. Cyril, incensed, made to rush at them but Cecil stopped him. "No, if you want Anne back you have to let this play out."

"But shouldn't we be doing something?"

"Like what, exactly? Call the local constabulary? No, he is more powerful than the Sun. We cannot win by strength, we can only win by protocol."

With a quick intake of breath Clemency yelled, "They're gone!"

"Quick!" said Cecil. "Back to the house, we must get in the way of the ceremony!"

Chapter Fourteen

The slick grass was making it difficult to run the short distance up the hill to the house. It felt an eternity running in sand. "Here," shouted Cyril pointing to a door hidden in the shadows of the house, "this door, it's a servant's entrance."

"What do we do now?" asked Clemency once inside, overheated and scared. There was little light to see.

Cecil inhaled, "I'm not actually sure." Clemency, for the first time detected a slight frisson of fear in his usually confident tone.

"Well, I'm getting Anne back," said Cyril. "No one, Prince of Darkness or not, can have my fiancée!"

"Well spoken, Cyril! Well spoken!" said Woolley rallying when suddenly from deep inside the house, came a terrible blood-curdling scream.

"Good God," moaned Cyril, "that's Anne. What is he doing to her?!"

Cecil took Clemency quickly in his arms and kissed her passionately. "Well, here's someone who's not going to wait to find out."

"Oh Woolley," she said.

"Where would I be without you?" he asked and they

kissed again. There was a second horrific scream.

Cyril shouted, "This way, Father's library is this way," and they raced off down the corridor.

As they turned the last corner nearest the library they were suddenly struck with an inability to move their limbs. "Woolley, I can't move!" Clemency screamed.

"Me neither," cried Cyril, terrified.

"I as well!" said Benedict.

"This is not real," shouted Cecil. "He's in our heads. He knows we are here and is playing with us. This is only a dream state. Fight it. You must fight it!"

The four wrenched and screamed trying to regain control while around them lights sputtered on and off, paintings fell, flowers wilted, objects shot about the hall; there was a horrid rotting smell.

Cecil concentrated all his effort. "I... can... just... move...." His feet felt lighter until at last he could advance. "I'm free! All of you... just tell yourself it is not real. Benedict, Cyril, Clemency... you must fight this!"

"Cecil, I can't, I can't...."

"You must."

"Oh, Cecil. I'll try... It's not real!... It's not real!... I'm doing it... It's not real!"

"Yes darling! Yes! And Cyril, you too! Say it! Say it for Anne!"

Cyril clenched his face, "This is not real! This is not real!" And suddenly he shot forward.

"Quick! Everyone...."

They ran down the hall and came to the library door only to find it covered by an entire wall of moss. "That devil!" Cecil hissed. "Quick, dig!" The four began to dig, pulling great clumps of earth and moss off the wall. The deeper they got, the wetter the earth became — wet and fetid and filled with crawling insects and worms. Clemency began to cry but refused to give up even as the smell of the earth grew fouler. Snakes and horrible many-eyed creatures pushed themselves out and fell onto the floor with wet slaps.

"How is this possible?!" exclaimed Cyril.

"He is the Prince of Darkness, he is the king of deception! Dig!"

"Oh my God, Woolley," Clemency screamed and grabbed hold of him. "It's a baby, it's a dead baby in the mud, in the wall. Oh, Woolley! Make it go away. Please… please… make it go away…."

Cyril hit something hard with his hands, "Ah! I've got to the door!" He tore at the remaining oozing fragments frantically. "There's no handle! No handle!"

Cecil stepped forward, "I know a trick or two also." He reached into his coat pocket pulled out a piece of chalk. He cleared a space large enough for his needs then drew three symbols. "Now, all of you, at the same time, knock three times on the count of three. One… two… three!"

They knocked.

The hall went black and silent. Deathly silent.

Cyril was the first to speak, "Did we do something right?"

"I think so, let me find my matches." Cecil struck a match and in the dim light they saw that everything was back to how it had been originally: no moss; no mud; no creatures; no dead babies. Cecil reached for the doorknob.

Chapter Fifteen

CECIL TURNED AND whispered, "Quiet now, I have no idea what we are going to find on the other side of this door. Let me go first and make sure it is safe…"

"Like hell you will! Anne is in there and I am going to…"

"No, Cyril, no heroes today. Remember who our foe is. You will lose and if you lose, so will she. This battle must be fought with our wits alone. Please, just wait here until I give the all clear."

Cecil slowly opened the door and as he did, a warm scented breeze came out that smelled of candle wax and dust, like a church. Cecil opened the door wider, cautiously peering in. The room was entirely filled with candles. There wasn't a surface that did not have a burning, glowing candle. The heat was stifling. The light was unnatural, a shadowy underwater state. Cecil motioned for the others to follow.

"Can you see Anne?" asked a distraught Cyril.

"No, this light makes it difficult to see anything distinctly. The shadows are too fantastic."

Clemency grabbed hold of Cecil's arm and pointed, "Oh, Cecil." For there lying on the floor was Anne, naked but for a series of symbols painted on her skin. She lay within the pentagram, her hands and feet horrifically nailed to the floor; blood was pooling around them. She was whimpering with pain, just barely alive.

Cyril rushed forward, "Oh God, darling!"

"Not so fast," said a voice from the darkness. "Not so fast." A slight but very tall figure stood out from the shadows. "Have we been introduced? You don't look familiar."

"I am Sir Clyde's son. Who in blazes are you?"

"Who in blazes, indeed… Good Lord, is that Cecil Herbert Woolley? I know your work, you've been keeping me on my toes." A long thin hand, more bone than flesh, with long black nails filed to a point extended out to Cecil. Cecil did not shake it. The gentleman seemed saddened but recovered and stiffened slightly. Turning to Cyril, he said, "I go by many names, I'm sure you know some." He stepped closer. The four were collectively disappointed by what they saw; a tall, thin man in a tweed suit with a pale, gaunt, pinched face, a long nose, thin lips and rather bushy eyebrows. "I do not know the lady, have we met?"

"I think not," said Clemency indignantly.

He paused. "Just a moment, you are Clemency de la Tour. What a thrill to meet you, I know your father slightly. Slightly." Clemency found the 'slightly' unpleasant sounding. He continued, "I am here, as you can see, on business. What brings you here?"

Cyril interrupted, "Good God man, that's my fiancée you've got there!"

"Fiancée, ah, Sir Clyde referred to her as his dividend. Are you saying she is flesh and blood? I found her thusly, nailed to the floor. Sir Clyde is a stickler for protocol."

"You beast, give her back to me," Cyril yelled.

The Prince of Darkness smiled. "I am confused. You see, I have business dealings with your father; he told me she was his property, his to use as trade. Are you saying you own this lovely girl?"

Cyril began shouting wildly, "Dammit, I don't own her! We are to be married. I love her, she is my fiancée."

"But you don't own her, is that correct? She is nothing to me, you see, though I do love her lovely red hair. And her hips. I have a thing for red hair and hipbones. So lovely and pale." He drifted and then collected himself, "She is merely... a dividend. Would you like to purchase her?"

Cyril became flustered. "What in blazes would I have to purchase her with that you don't already have?"

"Your soul, perhaps."

Cecil stepped forward. "Stop this! There will be no bartering for souls."

"Oh Mr. Woolley, this was getting interesting. There is nothing more fascinating than watching someone lose their soul... for love." He looked slyly over at Clemency. She blushed.

"No one is losing their soul today," replied Cecil. "I want you to give Anne back to us and get out of this house."

"Nothing would please me more, to be rid of all this red tape." He made a washing gesture with his hands. "It is Sir Clyde's soul that I want. Now that soul fascinates me. How corrupt and tainted it is. Think of all the lost lives, all the dashed hopes that lie within him... all seething and...." A secret panel opened and Sir Clyde fell into the room. "Why, Sir Clyde, we were just speaking of you, so kind of you to drop in. There seems to be a question of ownership of this dividend you so desperately offered to me."

Sir Clyde, shaking and glistening with sweat, stuttered, "Question? No. She is yours, yours I tell you. Take her. Take her. I need more time. More time I tell you. We talked about this. More time. I need to...."

"Enough, Sir Clyde! As much as I love to see grown men grovel, is she or is she not your property to give? I believe in contracts, binding contracts, and taking something that is not rightfully yours to pay a debt is... is, well, simply not done."

"She's my fiancée, dammit!" Cyril shouted, "and not related to Father in any way. Father, what have you done? What have you done!"

Sir Clyde shook himself, "Done? I've sent you to school, boy! I've kept this house running. Bought you books, a place in society. Paid for everything. Done? Money, son. Money keeps it all afloat."

"But Father, you sold your soul... for this?"

"At the time I didn't believe there were souls. Joke's on me I guess... but son, listen to me. Do you really know Anne that well? There'll be other girls, other opportunities — join me. We can be partners..."

"Father no! Stop this."

"I think we have our answer," the Prince said.

"No," screamed Sir Clyde. "Let me talk to him, he's a rational boy, let me... just give me some more time."

"Time is the one thing I have," the Prince said, putting his hand on Sir Clyde's shoulder, "and something you do not. It's been very pleasant meeting you. Mr. Woolley, I

hope we meet again soon. Clemency, so nice. Benedict…
what can I say? Goodbye. Come along Sir Clyde, payment
due." And with that, a cloud of acrid smoke shrouded the
room.

"Father! Father!" shouted Cyril desperately, but it was
too late, Sir Clyde was gone.

The room fell silent. Everyone stood dumbfounded,
unable to speak. Cecil, breaking the silence, cried out.
"Good God, Anne! Someone cover her! Anne, hold on,
we'll get those nails out!"

Chapter Sixteen

THE TRAIN SPED out of the Gare de l'Est, leaving behind a nighttime Paris that was just beginning its second wind. In their private sleeper couchette Cecil leaned over and took Clemency in his arms. "Darling, thank you for still wanting to be with me after all that. Was it too terrible?"

"Terrible, yes but I am ashamed to say that I loved it! How many people can boast that the Prince of Darkness knows your name? And we saved young love from the clutches of evil."

"That we did, darling."

"Oh, Cecil, do you really think that Cyril and Anne will be okay? How horrible to lose a father in such a gruesome way. And poor Anne, she looked so pale and weak in that hospital room."

"Those two are made of sturdy stuff." Cecil replied, taking off his jacket, "It's going to be hard for them to get over the shock but now that the dark cloud over Ravensend has lifted, there should be nothing but sweetness and light ahead for them."

"And for us," Clemency purred, kissing Cecil.

"Indeed, darling, indeed, but for us right now it's Shanghai or bust."

"Oh Cecil, why Shanghai? What's there that we cannot find in your apartment? Must we speed off to the other side of the earth when we could be in your bed, eating caviar and toast under the covers?"

"There is so much to see, so much I want to share with you — the Bund, Xin Tian Di, the Jade Buddha Temple, not to mention delicious cocktails, some of the best jazz that side of Paris and perhaps even a few ghosts."

"Ghosts? Hmm... just out of curiosity, is there a client attached to one of those Shanghai ghosts?"

"You are a clever one. But that is in six days. We have six glorious days alone on a train with as much caviar and toast as you want, six love-drenched days to begin new chapters in our autobiographies, six...."

There was a knock on the cabin door. "Open!" shouted Cecil. Benedict entered carrying a tray of martinis. "Why Benedict, you made it, I was worried."

"I regret causing you worry, sir, but there was no need. You clearly stated the time of departure."

"Yes, but I was more... the whole bigger picture... glad to see you... worried about your well-being... Oh never mind, you are here and Clemency is here — we are all here. Paris to Germany, Poland, Belarus, Russia and Shanghai!"

"And ghosts," added Clemency.

"Ghosts?" questioned Benedict.

"To ghosts!" toasted Cecil Herbert Woolley.

David Keyes is the author of over 15 books including *I Do So Worry For All Those Lost At Sea*, An Imagined Autobiography and *The Uninvited Guests,* the second book in the Cecil Herbert Woolley series.

Mr. Keyes is also a maker of clocks, curios and coffins as well as a composer, designer and photographer. He lives in Toronto with a number of cats and a skeleton named Basil.

Follow his adventures on Instagram @marlowghost

www.ingramcontent.com/pod-product-compliance
Lightning Source LLC
Chambersburg PA
CBHW070350130626
46556CB00007B/3120